America's Songs

AMERICA — the — BEAUTIFUL

Cavendish Square
New York

KRISTEN SUSIENKA

Published in 2020 by Cavendish Square Publishing, LLC
243 5th Avenue, Suite 136, New York, NY 10016

First Edition

Website: cavendishsq.com

Cataloging-in-Publication Data

Names: Susienka, Kristen.
Title: America the Beautiful / Kristen Susienka.
Description: New York : Cavendish Square Publishing, 2020. | Series:
America's songs | Includes glossary and index.
Identifiers: LCCN ISBN 9781502648617 (pbk.) | ISBN 9781502648631 (library bound) |
ISBN 9781502648624 (6pack) | ISBN 9781502648648 (ebook)
Subjects: LCSH: Bates, Katharine Lee, 1859-1929. America the beautiful--Juvenile literature. | Ward, Samuel A., 1847-1903. America the beautiful--Juvenile literature. | National songs--United States--History and criticism--Juvenile literature. | Patriotic music--United States--History and criticism--Juvenile literature.
Classification: LCC ML3551.S87 2020 | DDC 782.42'15990973--dc23

Editorial Director: David McNamara
Editor: Lauren Miller
Copy Editor: Nathan Heidelberger
Associate Art Director: Alan Sliwinski
Designer: Joe Parenteau
Production Coordinator: Karol Szymczuk
Photo Research: J8 Media

The photographs in this book are used by permission and through the courtesy of: Cover Ron Thomas/E+/Getty Images; p. 4 Michael Overstreet/iStock/Getty Images; p. 6 transcribed by Dr. Nathan Heidelberger; p. 8, 12 Heritage Auctions, HA.com; p. 12 Evelyn Hockstein/For The Washington Post/Getty Images; p. 14 William Henry Jackson/Library of Congress; p. 15 Corbis/Getty Images; p. 16 MPI/Getty Images; p. 18 Wikimedia Commons/File:Silas Gamaliel Pratt 1902.jpg/Public Domain; p, 19 The History Collection/Alamy Stock Photo; p. 22 Focus on Sport/Getty Images; p. 24 Pamela Au/Shutterstock.com; p. 25 Kevin Terrell/AP Images; p. 27 Linda Cataffo/NY Daily News Archive/Getty Images.

Printed in the United States of America

CONTENTS

Chapter 1

More Than a Beautiful Song 5

Sheet Music 6

Chapter 2

Writing "America the Beautiful" 13

Timeline 20

Chapter 3

The Song's Importance Today 23

Glossary 28

Find Out More 29

Index 31

About the Author 32

Many famous songs about America talk about the country's beautiful scenes of nature, including forests, mountains, and rivers.

CHAPTER 1

More Than a Beautiful Song

The United States is a large and beautiful country. It has mountains, lakes, rivers, forests, and deserts. Many people visit it every year.

Today, people take pictures of their favorite places in America. Before cameras and phones could take pictures, people wrote about or painted what

America the Beautiful

Lyrics by Katharine Lee Bates

Music by Samuel Augustus Ward

O beautiful for pilgrim feet,
Whose stern, impassioned stress
A thoroughfare of freedom beat
Across the wilderness!
America! America!
God mend thine every flaw,
Confirm thy soul in self-control,
Thy liberty in law!

O beautiful for heroes proved
In liberating strife,
Who more than self their country loved,
And mercy more than life!
America! America!
May God thy gold refine,
Till all success be nobleness,
And every gain divine!

O beautiful for patriot dream
That sees beyond the years
Thine alabaster cities gleam
Undimmed by human tears!
America! America!
God shed His grace on thee
And crown thy good with brotherhood
From sea to shining sea!

they saw. Many **patriotic** songs were poems first. One famous example is "America the Beautiful."

Katharine Lee Bates loved writing and teaching. She also published several books, including children's books.

A Beautiful Poem

In 1893, Katharine Lee Bates wrote the poem "America the Beautiful." She wanted to celebrate the beauty she saw around her. The poem paints a picture of a place full of pretty

FACT

Some people think "America the Beautiful" should be the national anthem. They think "America the Beautiful" is easier to sing. They also like that it talks more about America's beauty.

What Does It Mean?

"America the Beautiful" is a song with many meanings. Above all, it is a song about loving America. It first talks about America's beautiful sights ("spacious skies"). Next it talks about how people came to America and explored it ("pilgrim's feet ... across the wilderness"). Then it talks about hope for the country's future ("patriot dream / that sees beyond the years"). For many, it is a song of hope. It helps people remember what makes America a good country.

Words to Know

alabaster White.
amber waves of grain Fields of wheat.
brotherhood Friendship, or being close like family.
in liberating strife In difficult times.
thee An old-fashioned way of saying "you."
thoroughfare A long street.
thy An old-fashioned way of saying "your."

skies, tall mountains, and waving fields of wheat. When people first read the poem, they liked it a lot. The words reminded them of the beautiful places

A band dressed in costumes from the American Revolution performs patriotic songs during a Fourth of July celebration in Washginton, DC, in 2014. Many bands play "America the Beautiful" every Fourth of July.

where they lived. They shared the poem with other people. Later, the poem became a song. People sang it because they liked the song's message.

The song is popular to sing. Sometimes bands play it at parades. Some people have changed the words to the song to fit different events going on in their lives. Other people still prefer the song's original words and message. It is a song that will continue to be important to America for years to come.

> **FACT**
> Sometimes people sing the song after a sad event happens. Opera singer Denyce Graves sang it during a **memorial service** in 2001. The service was held to honor everyone who died in the September 11, 2001, terrorist attacks.

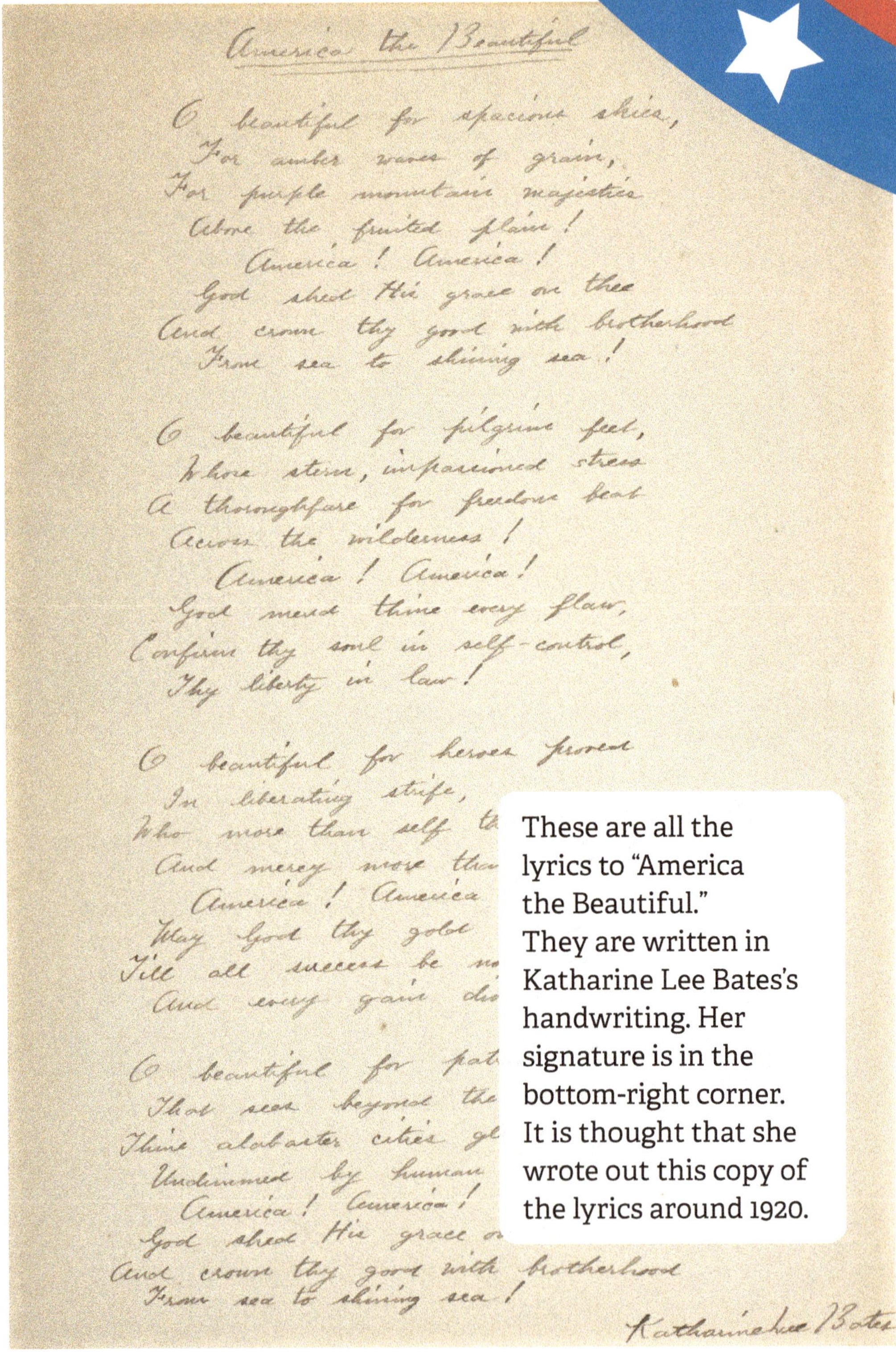

America the Beautiful

O beautiful for spacious skies,
For amber waves of grain,
For purple mountain majesties
Above the fruited plain!
America! America!
God shed His grace on thee
And crown thy good with brotherhood
From sea to shining sea!

O beautiful for pilgrim feet,
Whose stern, impassioned stress
A thoroughfare for freedom beat
Across the wilderness!
America! America!
God mend thine every flaw,
Confirm thy soul in self-control,
Thy liberty in law!

O beautiful for heroes proved
In liberating strife,
Who more than self th
And mercy more th
America! America
May God thy gold
Till all success be n
And every gain di

O beautiful for pat
That sees beyond the
Thine alabaster cities gl
Undimmed by human
America! America!
God shed His grace o
And crown thy good with brotherhood
From sea to shining sea!

Katharine Lee Bates

These are all the lyrics to "America the Beautiful." They are written in Katharine Lee Bates's handwriting. Her signature is in the bottom-right corner. It is thought that she wrote out this copy of the lyrics around 1920.

CHAPTER 2

Writing "America the Beautiful"

"America the Beautiful" has an interesting history. It goes back over 125 years, when Katharine Lee Bates was traveling across America's beautiful countryside and enjoying the tall mountains of the **American West**.

What Was the World Like?

Katharine Lee Bates was an English **professor** in Massachusetts. In 1893, she was asked to come to Colorado to teach. She took trains to get there. She

This old photograph shows a Colorado valley. You can see Pikes Peak in the background.

saw many mountains, lakes, fields, and forests on the journey. She was inspired by what she saw. The first words to "America the Beautiful" are "O beautiful for spacious skies." They were written after Bates and some friends climbed part of a mountain in Colorado. The mountain was named Pikes Peak. The rest of the song was inspired by what Bates saw on her way to Colorado and while she lived there.

In the 1800s, America grew. It gained the American West in 1803. People explored the West. They wrote about its beautiful **landscapes**. In the 1850s, people wanted to find

FACT

Pikes Peak was named after explorer Zebulon Pike. He tried to climb to the top in 1806. It was too snowy to climb all the way up, though.

This drawing shows the explorer Zebulon Pike.

Many paintings tried to show the American West's beauty. This painting is called *Barlow Cutoff*. It was painted in 1865 by William Henry Jackson. It illustrates a landscape in Oregon.

gold in the West's mountains. Some people did. Other people didn't. However, many people stayed in the West. They built new towns and cities. They inspired people like Bates to visit.

In Bates's time, many people traveled to see the West's forests, mountains, and deserts. Some people wanted to make these places into big cities. Others worried that lots of people moving there could destroy the natural beauty. Bates and many other people wanted to protect the beautiful landscapes. They wrote poems and books, or painted pictures of the West. Bates's poem inspired others to appreciate and protect the country's landscapes.

Becoming a Song

"America the Beautiful" was first published in a Christian newspaper in 1895. A new version was published a Boston, Massachusetts, newspaper in 1904. Bates added the song's final words in 1913.

As soon as it was published in 1895, the poem became popular in the United States. After a few months, some people liked the poem so much they wanted to make it into a song. A man named

Silas G. Pratt was the first person to write music for the poem "America the Beautiful." Here he is in 1902.

Silas G. Pratt wrote music for it. Others matched the words to different popular songs. In 1926, a group called the National Federation of Music Clubs supported a contest to write new music for the poem. However, no one won the contest. Instead, the National Federation of Music Clubs chose music written by a man named Samuel Augustus Ward.

Who Wrote the Song's Music?

"America the Beautiful" has two **composers**. The song's first composer was Silas G. Pratt. He wrote music for the poem in 1895. In 1926, a new **melody** was chosen. Samuel Augustus Ward wrote the music. It was not for "America the Beautiful," though. Ward had written the music for a **hymn** called "O Mother Dear, Jerusalem" in 1882. His melody went well with the words of "America the Beautiful." People liked its easy tune. Today, the song "America the Beautiful" is sung with Ward's music.

FACT

Before it got its own music, one melody that worked well with the words of "America the Beautiful" was "Auld Lang Syne." This song is usually sung on New Year's Eve.

Samuel Augustus Ward wrote his tune in 1882.

Timeline

1806 Zebulon Pike visits Colorado and tries to climb to the top of Pikes Peak. Due to snowy weather, he eventually abandons the attempt.

1800s–1870s The United States gains land in the West from France and Mexico. Some people move there looking for gold. Others move to start farms or businesses.

1882 Samuel Augustus Ward writes the melody for a sixteenth-century hymn called "O Mother Dear, Jerusalem." It eventually becomes the melody for "America the Beautiful."

1890 The beautiful area of Yosemite in California becomes a national park.

1893 Katharine Bates travels to Colorado for work. While in Colorado, she writes the poem "America the Beautiful."

- **December 1893** Chicago holds the World's Fair. Many inventors and visitors attend the fair.
- **1895** Bates publishes the first version of her poem. Silas G. Pratt writes the first music for "America the Beautiful."
- **1913** Bates writes the final words of "America the Beautiful."
- **1914–1918** World War I is fought.
- **1926** The National Federation of Music Clubs holds a contest to come up with a new melody for "America the Beautiful." No song entries win. Samuel Ward's melody to "O Mother Dear, Jerusalem" is chosen instead.
- **1929** Katharine Bates dies.

Famous singers like John Legend have sung the song. Here, he is singing at Super Bowl XLIX in 2015.

CHAPTER 3

The Song's Importance Today

"America the Beautiful" is still sung today. It is an important song for many US citizens. People use the song in several ways. Some people like to sing it to remember happy moments. Others sing it to comfort each other. Many famous people have sung the song too.

Where Is the Song Sung Today?

The song is sung or played at Fourth of July parades every year. Churches also play the song at church services around that time. The Fourth of July celebrates America's independence. It is also an important day for "America the Beautiful." Katharine

Members of the US military march in parades on Veterans Day. Here, service members walk during a Veterans Day parade in Arizona in 2016.

Lee Bates published the song in a Christian newspaper called the *Congregationalist* on July 4, 1895.

> **FACT**
> After the bombing of Pearl Harbor in 1941, "America the Beautiful" was sung outside the White House.

Veterans Day is another important time in America. It takes place on November 11 every year. This day celebrates people who fought in all wars around the world. During events on Veterans Day, "America the Beautiful" might be played.

This woman is signing words to the song. She is signing "brotherhood" here.

Not only is the song sung by people or played by bands. It has also been translated into American Sign Language. People who are deaf can sign the words to the song.

FACT

"America the Beautiful" is sung at the opening of every WrestleMania event. Many well-known singers have sung the song at the event. Aretha Franklin, John Legend, and Fifth Harmony are examples.

A Song for the Future

"America the Beautiful" became very popular after people first read Katharine Bates's words. Today, it is one of the best-known American songs. It helps people care about the country. It also helps people care about each other. It is a song that will always have a special meaning to Americans everywhere.

Who Sang It Best?

Some of the best performances of "America the Beautiful" have happened in modern times. In 2001, a singer named Ray Charles sang it at the Super Bowl halftime show. His version was different and slower than the traditional tune. People loved it.

Then, in September that year, New York City and Washington, DC, were attacked by terrorists. After the attacks, the American people got together to express their sadness and hope for the future. One way they did this was by singing patriotic songs like "America the Beautiful."

Musician Ray Charles liked to sing "America the Beautiful" at sports events. Here he performs it at a World Series baseball game in 2001.

In 2005 and 2013, singer Mariah Carey performed the song at a Fourth of July concert in New York City's Liberty Park. Many others have sung the song at other events, but these versions are most memorable.

GLOSSARY

American West The part of the United States that is west of the Mississippi River.

composer A person who writes music.

hymn A song usually about God and sung in church.

landscapes The natural features of a place, like trees, mountains, and lakes.

melody The main part in a piece of music that people sing.

memorial service An event where people remember others who have died.

patriotic Relating to love of a country.

professor A person who teaches college classes.

FIND OUT MORE

Books

Bates, Katharine, et. al. *America the Beautiful: Together We Stand*. New York: Orchard Books, 2013.

Bates, Katharine Lee, and Kate Melrose. *My America, the Beautiful*. Sanger, CA: Familius, 2018.

Ponder, Melinda M. *Katharine Lee Bates: From Sea to Shining Sea*. Chicago: Windy City Publishers, 2017.

Websites

National Institute of Environmental Health Sciences: Patriotic Songs

https://kids.niehs.nih.gov/games/songs/patriotic/index.htm

This website introduces students, parents, and teachers to patriotic songs. It also offers examples of song activities kids can do.

Songwriters Hall of Fame: Katharine Lee Bates

https://www.songhall.org/profile/Katharine_Lee_Bates

Here, read about Katharine Lee Bates's life before and after she wrote "America the Beautiful."

Videos

"America the Beautiful" by Ray Charles

https://www.youtube.com/watch?v=3qtIknAoX78

Watch legendary singer Ray Charles sing "America the Beautiful" at the 2001 Super Bowl halftime show.

Kiboomers: "America the Beautiful"

https://www.youtube.com/watch?v=ONpP0isJMsY

With this video, you can watch and listen to the song's words being sung.

INDEX

Page numbers in **boldface** refer to images. Entries in **boldface** are glossary terms.

American Sign Language, 25, **25**
American West, 13–17, **14**, **16**, 20
Bates, Katharine Lee, 8, **8**, **12**, 13–17, 20–21, 24–26
beauty of nature, 5, 7–11, 13, 15–17
Carey, Mariah, 27
Charles, Ray, 27, 27
composer, 18–19, **18**, **19**
famous performances, 11, 25–27, **27**
Fourth of July, **10**, 24–25, 27
Franklin, Aretha, 26
gold, 15–16, 20
hymn, 19–20
landscapes, **4**, **14**, 15–17, **16**
Legend, John, **22**, 26
lyrics (complete), 6–7, **12**
meaning of song, 8–11, 15
melody, 6, 19–21
memorial service, 11
national anthem, 8
"O Mother Dear, Jerusalem," 19–21
parades, **10**, 11, 24, **24**
patriotic, 8, 27
Pikes Peak, **14**, 15, 20
Pratt, Silas G., 17–19, **18**, 21
professor, 14
September 11 attacks, 11, 27
sheet music, 6
Veterans Day, **24**, 25
Ward, Samuel Augustus, 18–21, **19**

ABOUT THE AUTHOR

Kristen Susienka earned her bachelor's in English from St. Norbert College in De Pere, Wisconsin. She later received her master's in publishing. She is an avid reader, writer, and runner living in Western New York. One of her favorite things to do is sing. She also loves learning about songs of the past.